PUFFIN BOOKS

Published by the Penguin Group
Penguin Books Ltd, 80 Strand, London WC2R 0RL, England
Penguin Group (USA) Inc., 375 Hudson Street, New York, New York 10014, USA
Penguin Group (Canada), 90 Eglinton Avenue East, Suite 700, Toronto, Ontario, Canada M4P 2Y3
(a division of Pearson Penguin Canada Inc.)
Penguin Ireland, 25 St Stephen's Green, Dublin 2, Ireland (a division of Penguin Books Ltd)
Penguin Group (Australia), 250 Camberwell Road, Camberwell, Victoria 3124, Australia
(a division of Pearson Australia Group Pty Ltd)
Penguin Books India Pvt Ltd, 11 Community Centre, Panchsheel Park, New Delhi – 110 017, India
Penguin Group (NZ), 67 Apollo Drive, Mairangi Bay, Auckland 1310, New Zealand
(a division of Pearson New Zealand Ltd)
Penguin Books (South Africa) (Pty) Ltd, 24 Sturdee Avenue, Rosebank, Johannesburg 2196, South Africa

Penguin Books Ltd, Registered Offices: 80 Strand, London WC2R 0RL, England

penguin.com

First published in the USA by HarperCollins 2007
First published in Great Britain by Puffin Books 2007
1 3 5 7 9 10 8 6 4 2

Copyright © Paramount Pictures Corp., 2007
All rights reserved

Made and printed in Trento, Italy

British Library Cataloguing in Publication Data
A CIP catalogue record for this book is available from the British Library

ISBN: 978–0–141–32146–2

Charlotte's Web

The Perfect Word

Adapted by Catherine Hapka

Based on the Motion Picture Screenplay by

Susanna Grant & Karey Kirkpatrick

Based on the book by E. B. White

PUFFIN

Templeton the rat lived by his own rules. And his number-one rule was: every rat for himself.

But when Wilbur the pig came to the barn, things started to change.

First Wilbur made friends with Charlotte the spider.
Before long he was friends with everyone – even Templeton.

But then something terrible happened. Templeton accidentally told Wilbur a secret: come Christmastime, Wilbur would be turned into sausages and bacon!

Charlotte knew she had to save her friend from the terrible fate he'd been told. She just didn't know how to. Then . . . she had an idea.

She did what she did best. She spun a beautiful web with the words "Some Pig" in it.

People came from all over town to see the web. That saved Wilbur . . . for a while. But soon Charlotte needed more words to spin.

That was where Templeton came in.

"That rat is always drag-drag-dragging in rubbish with writing on it," Gussy the goose pointed out.

At first Templeton refused to help. But then he realized something: having a pig around meant lots of scraps for him to eat.

So off he went to the dump to find more words to save Wilbur.

A pair of crows sat on a sign. They spotted Templeton scurrying towards the mounds of rubbish.

"Want to go mess with him?" one crow asked.

"Sounds like fun," the other replied.

The crows cawed and dive-bombed Templeton. He darted into an empty tin, just in time.

"The rat is not enjoying this!" Templeton muttered. He was almost ready to give up.

Finally the crows flew away. Templeton spotted a newspaper.

"Hey, look," he said. "Words."

He ripped off a piece of the newspaper and carried it back to the barn.

Charlotte used the word "radiant" from the newspaper. And again, people came from all over to see her miraculous web.

But then Mr Zuckerman decided to take Wilbur to the County Fair. If Wilbur didn't win a prize, he would be turned into dinner after all!

Charlotte couldn't let that happen. She needed another word.

Once again, Templeton refused to help. "What's in it for the rat?" he asked.

The geese told him exactly what was in it for him: food! At the fair there would be sticky, greasy, half-eaten glorious food everywhere he looked!

Templeton and Charlotte snuck along to the fair.

"Get me some words by nightfall," Charlotte told Templeton. "Please."

"You do realize I'm just here for the food, right?" Templeton grumbled.

But he went out and found more words for Charlotte.

Wilbur looked on as she worked all night to spin another web.

Templeton looked up at the word in the web: "humble".

Wilbur may not have been the biggest or the best-looking pig at the fair, but he certainly had heart.

It was the perfect word. Thanks to the rat (and a very kind spider), everyone, including the judges, would know how special Wilbur was. He really was some radiant, humble pig!